# Mr Wellington Boots

## Three magical cat stories

"Oh, poor little thing!" said Selina's mum. She picked up the cat and brushed off the dust from its fur.

The poor little thing smiled a sneaky cat-smile, and thought it might stay if the food was all right.

"Isn't he lovely?" said Selina. "Can we keep him? I'll call him Mr Wellington Boots."

"Whatever for?" said Peter.

"Because he's got them on," said Selina.

ANN RUFFELL

# Mr Wellington Boots

## Three magical cat stories

Illustrated by Jan Lewis

For Selina and her friends.

Scholastic Children's Books,
Commonwealth House, 1–19 New Oxford Street,
London WC1A 1NU, UK
a division of Scholastic Ltd
London ~ New York ~ Toronto ~ Sydney ~ Auckland

Published in the UK by Scholastic Ltd, 1996

Text copyright © Ann Ruffell, 1996
Illustrations copyright © Jan Lewis, 1996

ISBN 0 590 13544 9

Typeset by Contour Typesetters, Southall, London
Printed by Cox & Wyman Ltd, Reading, Berkshire

10 9 8 7 6 5

# 1. The White Elephant Stall

## Chapter 1

Mr Wellington Boots was a witch's cat, only nobody knew. Selina, her mum and dad and her brother Peter had found Mr Wellington Boots outside one day. He was yowling very noisily.

"Oh, poor little thing!" said Selina's mum. She picked up the cat and brushed off the dust from its fur.

The poor little thing smiled a sneaky cat-smile, and thought it might stay if the food was all right.

"Isn't he lovely?" said Selina. "Can we keep him? I'll call him Mr Wellington Boots."

"Whatever for?" said Peter.

"Because he's got them on," said Selina.

That was why they didn't know he was a witch's cat. Instead of being all black, he was only black up to his knees. The rest of him was a nice, smoky grey.

"Bring him inside," said Mum. "We'll get him a saucer of milk and ask around to see if anyone owns him."

But of course nobody came to say they owned him. His witch had gone off for a long holiday to a Very Black Forest and left him to look after himself.

Mr Wellington Boots smiled his sneaky cat-smile and slurped up all the milk. Then he put on a hungry look and tipped his head on one side.

"Give him some of the liver we've got for tea," said Selina. She hated liver.

Mr Wellington Boots smiled another sneaky cat-smile. The old witch had only given him old fish heads to eat. So he moved in and lived royally on real tinned cat food and the occasional lump of teatime liver.

Soon after this there was going to be a Garden Fête in the school grounds.

Selina had never been to a Garden Fête before.

"It's a sort of market with stalls," said Mum. "Only it's better because you know the people on the stalls."

"It's a sort of party with lots of things to do," said Dad. "Only it's better because you don't have to do them if you don't want to."

"It's a waste of a good Saturday," said Peter. "And a waste of good pocket money."

"But I'm going to help Mum on one of the stalls," said Selina. "It's the White Elephant stall."

Selina had never seen a white elephant before. She'd only seen an ordinary grey elephant once, at the zoo.

"Why don't you want to help on the White Elephant stall?" she asked Peter.

Peter was going to help Dad with the clock golf instead. "You're not scared of white elephants, are you?"

Peter laughed very noisily. "Don't you know?" he said. "White Elephant stalls don't sell white elephants!"

"What do they sell, then, Mister Clever?" said Selina.

"Old rubbish!" giggled Peter.

Selina knew he was quite wrong, but she asked her mum, just to make sure.

"That's right," said Mum. "A White Elephant stall is full of things people don't want. Like white elephants."

"Why don't people want white elephants?" demanded Selina. "I'd like a white elephant."

"Out in the wild, they'd stand out against

the grey ones," said Mum. "The rest of the herd don't want them because they get noticed and hunters might come along and shoot them all."

"That's true," said Dad, "but I know a different story. In India white elephants are very special. In fact, they're so special that people used to give them away as presents. But you need a lot of room for an elephant, and they're expensive to keep. They're not like cats."

Mr Wellington Boots gave a satisfied purr.

Dad finished his story. "So though you were supposed to be grateful, most people didn't want to be given a white elephant for a present."

"I wouldn't mind if someone gave me one," said Selina.

Mr Wellington Boots began thinking, but he said nothing.

## Chapter 2

On Saturday Selina woke up early. She couldn't wait for things to start happening.

"Why are mornings so long when you're waiting for something to happen?" she asked Mr Wellington Boots. "I do wish Peter hadn't told me there aren't any real white elephants on a White Elephant stall. I was looking forward to them."

Mr Wellington Boots golloped away at tinned tuna. He thought he might as well do a bit of cat-witchery, just to cheer Selina up.

At last it was time to go and set up Dad's clock golf and get the White Elephant stall ready. The Garden Fête was going to open at two o'clock, and there was a lot to do before then.

There were lots of mums and dads and teachers on the school field. They unpacked boxes and cases and carried heaps of stuff across the grass. Nobody saw the grey and black cat crawling under a stall.

Mrs Speed next door came up to Selina. She was carrying a box.

"Something for you, Selina. You're on the White Elephant stall, aren't you?"

"Yes," said Selina, and held out her arms for the box. She nearly didn't bother to look inside because she was sure it was going to be something very boring. Something nobody wanted. Only there was a funny, snuffly sort of sound, and the box moved in her arms.

Mr Wellington Boots gave a cat laugh under the stall.

Selina peeped inside the box.

It was a very small, very baby white elephant, about as big as a piglet, with blue eyes and very shiny toenails.

Mum turned round and jumped when she saw it. "You can't put that animal on my stall," she said.

"Why not? It's a white elephant," said Selina.

"I suppose it is," said Mum. "All right. Only don't let it be a nuisance. I'd better get some straw from Daddy's clock golf."

Dad had edged his game with bales of straw to stop the golf balls rolling too far.

"I thought elephants ate buns," said Selina.

"Hay, and leaves and vegetables," said Mum. "Only it will have to make do with straw because that's all we've got. Keep it away from the Garden stall. I don't want us to get into trouble because it's eaten all the tomato plants!"

Several other people came to Selina's stall with their white elephants. She knew then that Peter and Mum and Dad had been quite wrong. A White Elephant stall was exactly what it said it was.

"Oh, my goodness," said Mum when she came back with a bag of straw. "I think we're going to need a bit more straw than this. What are we going to do with them all?"

"Sell them," said Selina.

"But nobody wants white elephants," said Mum.

"I do," said Selina, and stroked the very small, very baby elephant with the blue eyes and the very shiny toenails.

## Chapter 3

Selina's White Elephant stall became very crowded. There were tall ones, small ones and middle-sized ones. All of them were white except for one very old one that was a bit grey about the ears.

It had been brought by Mr Attfield across the road, and it began to cause trouble right away. It didn't want to stand tidily with the other elephants. It had been boss in the far off place where it had once lived, and it wasn't going to stop being boss now.

It lifted up its trunk and let out a terrific scream.

Selina and her mum and Mr Attfield and everyone else nearby put their hands over their ears.

"Naughty elephant," scolded Selina when it had finished. "Just behave yourself."

Mr Attfield's elephant put its trunk down. Nobody had ever spoken to it like that before.

It lifted its trunk again to give another scream, but Selina told it off again. "I'm ashamed of you," she said. "You're the oldest elephant here. You should set an example. Stop behaving like a baby."

Mr Attfield's elephant hung its head. Its grey ears began to glow red. Old bossy elephants don't usually get scolded by small girls.

It turned its head and walked away so that nobody should see it. Unfortunately it walked behind the Smash-a-plate stall.

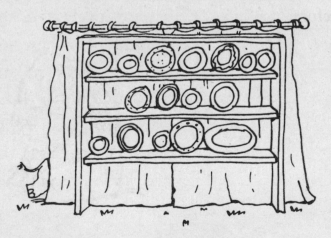

Selina's friend Hannah was arranging the old plates on a shelf. It was a lovely stall. You got three balls for your money, then you could throw them as hard as you liked and smash as many plates as you liked.

The old white elephant didn't know this. It poked its trunk through the canvas at the back. Hannah screamed, and ran to tell her dad.

Hannah's dad began to run. He was too late. Mr Attfield's elephant had knocked down four shelves full of old plates. It had knocked down the four shelves as well.

"We're not even open yet!" shouted Hannah.

"I'm very sorry," said Selina. "Can I help you put the shelves back?"

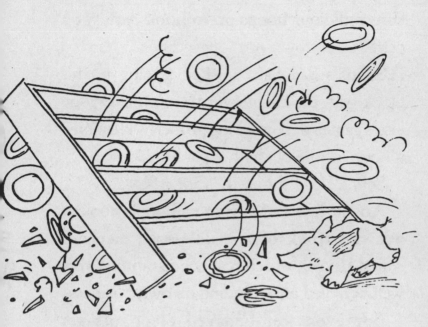

"I'll do it," said Hannah's dad. "Just you keep that elephant away from here."

By now the other elephants were getting out of hand. It was all Dad's fault, really.

This is what happened.

The White Elephant stall was right next to the Hoopla stall. Peter's best friend Tim was busy hanging hooks in difficult places. If you threw all your hoops on to hooks you got a prize.

Selina's dad had finished setting up his clock golf. He came over to see if everyone else's games were working properly. He aimed a hoop at one of the hoopla hooks.

Selina's dad shouted, "Got it!"

And he had. But it wasn't a hoopla hook. It was the trunk of a middle-sized elephant called Hooky, which had been standing very well behaved and minding its own business.

But even well-behaved elephants get startled when someone throws a hoopla hoop over their trunks.

Hooky galloped off in panic. As he went he knocked over a pile of coconuts waiting to be put on to stands for the coconut-shy.

The coconuts rolled all over the place. Children jumped over them as they rolled. Mums and dads carrying things didn't see them. They rolled over the rolling coconuts and dropped their pot plants, hockey sticks and boxes of cakes. Another lot of mums and dads fell over the pot plants and hockey sticks. Some of the children thought it was a good idea to try out the cakes.

Mr Wellington Boots opened his eyes under the White Elephant stall. He smiled a sneaky cat-smile. Everything was happening just as he had planned.

Then he saw Selina. She was the only person trying to catch Hooky.

Mr Wellington Boots sneezed. Hooky waved his trunk, wondering why he was there, then turned round and came back to Selina's stall.

"Phew! We're all ready now," said Selina. "It's nearly two o'clock."

Mr Wellington Boots smiled another sneaky cat-smile and went back to sleep.

# Chapter 4

Selina made Hooky stand at the back of the stall. The elephants were all in rows so that they could be seen properly.

At two o'clock Mrs Pope, the head-mistress, opened the Garden Fête. Selina had to keep her elephants quiet. It would be awful if they ruined Mrs Pope's speech by trumpeting too loudly.

After the speech everyone came to buy things from the stalls and Selina's proper job started.

"How much, Selina?" asked Mrs Pope, patting Hooky on the trunk.

Selina looked at the label Mum had stuck on him. "Fifty pence, please," she said.

Mrs Pope handed Selina the money.

# YOUNG HIPPO

# READERS' CLUB

## The sign of good storytelling!

**Introductory Price £4.99 WORTH £12.98**

Now you can build your own library of magical, spooky, adventurous and funny Young Hippo tales!

Young Hippo books contain brilliantly written stories by well-known authors, which will stimulate an interest in reading both at home and at school. These highly collectable books are perfect for children who have begun to read full length stories for themselves.

Your introductory pack will be delivered to your home in about 28 days. If for any reason you aren't completely satisfied, just return it to us for a full refund. Then, with no obligation, and for as long as you want, each month we will send you another exciting pack of three books plus a brilliant free gift for only £6.99 (saving pounds on the published price). You can cancel at any time. Send this coupon to the address below with your Parent's/Guardian's signature, with only £4.99 today!

YOUNG HIPPO Magic — The Wishing Horse — Malcolm Yorke

YOUNG HIPPO Funny — Count Draco Down Under

YOUNG HIPPO School — Whizz Bang and the Crocodile Room

**DELIVERED FREE TO YOUR HOME**

**Your introductory pack will contain:** • Whizz Bang and the Crocodile Room • The Wishing Horse • Count Draco Down Under • and a Hippo Glove Puppet

Then a very strange thing happened. As Mrs Pope walked away with her elephant on a string, the animal seemed to shrink. Its ears, instead of hanging down like mud flaps, stuck upwards and grew points. Its feet stuck together and the toenails turned into round, wooden wheels.

It wasn't an elephant any more. It was a wooden horse with its tail missing.

Underneath the stall, Mr Wellington Boots yawned a wide, pink yawn, and smiled his sneaky cat-smile. He curled up in the other direction and went back to sleep.

"Just the thing for the school nursery," said Mrs Pope, delighted.

Then more people came queuing up to buy a white elephant.

And the odd thing was, each elephant turned into something that person really wanted – a lampshade, or a basket of hair-slides, a half-full bottle of scent, or a jigsaw with only two pieces missing.

At the end of the Garden Fête, there was only one white elephant left.

It was the one Mrs Speed had brought, the first one on the stall. The one that was just the size of a piglet, with blue eyes and shiny toenails.

Selina turned to Mum who was counting the money they had taken on their stall.

"I haven't spent any of my pocket money," she said. "Do you think...?"

Mum looked at the small white elephant with the shiny toenails. It had behaved beautifully all day.

"Are you sure?" said Mum.

"Quite sure," said Selina. She tied a string round the small elephant's neck and said, "Come on, it's time to go home."

The small white elephant lifted its trunk and gave a funny, snuffly kind of sound. Under the stall Mr Wellington Boots woke up properly and decided it was time he went home too.

When Selina led the little white elephant away everybody watched. But it didn't turn into a vase, or a pair of matching book-ends, or even a set of coat-hangers. It stayed a very small white elephant with blue eyes and very shiny toenails.

Mr Wellington Boots smiled a very sneaky cat-smile and jumped on to the elephant's back. He wasn't going to walk home if he could help it.

# 2. The Zoo Thief

## Chapter 1

Selina's elephant grew. He still had blue eyes and shiny toenails, but he was not small any more. She called him Hank, because he was as big and white as one of Dad's hankies.

Now he was too big to keep at home.

"Don't worry," said Dad. "We'll ask the zoo to look after him. I'll help you write a letter."

A few days later a reply came from the zoo. This is what it said:

Appledown Zoo

Dear Selina,

We would be very pleased to look after your white elephant. We have no elephants of this colour in our zoo. We will arrange collection next Monday.

Yours sincerely,

J. Hackett, Director.

On Monday a very large horsebox arrived outside Selina's house. "It's our special elephant transporter," said the driver.

"You could get ten of our elephant in that," said Dad, and called Selina to bring Hank out from the shed.

"He's not very big," said the driver.

"He's too big for our house," said Dad.

"I can see that," said the driver. "But he'll rattle about in there."

Hank could smell delicious new hay at the back of the elephant transporter. He ran up the ramp with no trouble at all.

Mr Wellington Boots wondered what all the fuss was about, and slipped inside the elephant transporter too. The driver didn't see the cat go inside. He barred the door.

"Can I go with him?" asked Selina.

"Sure. Hop in," said the driver.

So Dad and Selina hopped in the front.

At the zoo Dad and Selina hopped out. So did Mr Wellington Boots. Nobody saw him because he slid straight under the booth which says PAY HERE.

The keepers came to meet Hank.

"We've never had a white one before," said one of them.

Selina had to ask the keepers a question. "Will Hank be quite safe? Will the rest of the herd try to get rid of him because he's white?"

The elephant keeper was quite sure they wouldn't. "He would only be dangerous to them in the wild," he explained. "They're all safe here in the zoo."

Selina met the other elephants. They sniffed at Hank, and Hank sniffed back. Then they went off together to find some hay.

The elephant house was warm and cosy, and they had a big field to walk about in. There were plenty of people to look at, and there was plenty of hay to eat and plenty of straw to sleep on.

Mr Wellington Boots explored the zoo. He thought it was cold and draughty. Hay and straw were prickly. He preferred Mum's chair or Selina's bed. And the food didn't look so good. He went back to the PAY HERE booth to wait for Selina.

"I think Hank will be very happy here," said Selina, "but I'm going to miss him like anything."

"You can come and help whenever you like," said the keeper. "We always need people to clean the cages and feed the animals."

Mr Wellington Boots listened from under the PAY HERE booth. He thought he might as well come to the zoo with Selina a few times. He wasn't going to clean cages and feed animals, but he might find some fish to eat in the penguin pool.

They had to take the bus home from the zoo.

Mr Wellington Boots came out from the PAY HERE booth just in time.

"Look!" said Dad. "There's a cat just like Mr Wellington Boots!"

"It *is* Mr Wellington Boots," said Selina. "How did you get here, Boots?"

Mr Wellington Boots tried to tell her, but nobody listened. The zoo keeper found a cardboard box to put him in.

"You can't have a cat running wild in a bus," said the keeper.

Mr Wellington Boots tried to tell everyone that you *could* have cats running wild in a bus, but nobody listened. They tied the box up with string.

He ran round and round the box in the bus, just to prove you could have cats running wild in a bus. Dad and Selina were very glad he was inside the box.

## Chapter 2

Selina went to the zoo every Saturday and Sunday to look after Hank and to tell him that she hadn't forgotten him. Hank was happy with his new friends in the zoo, but he was even happier when Selina came to visit him.

Dad bought a special basket for Mr Wellington Boots to travel in when they went on the bus. He grew very fat on fish.

One day there was a new keeper in the children's zoo. He was cleaning out the chinchilla rabbits' cage.

Selina was surprised. She thought she knew all the keepers in the zoo. This one must be a new one.

She was just going to go up and say "Hello", when she saw a strange thing. The new keeper suddenly picked up a chinchilla rabbit and stuffed it under his coat.

No wonder she didn't know this keeper. He wasn't a keeper at all. He was stealing the rabbits!

Selina thought she knew why. People make fur coats out of chinchilla rabbit fur. If he sold them, he would get a lot of money.

There was nobody about. Most of the real keepers had gone off for their tea. All the visitors had gone to watch the sea lions being fed.

She had to do something by herself.

Mr Wellington Boots was very full of the penguins' fish. He curled himself round her legs.

"Good old Boots," she whispered. "You'll help, won't you?"

Mr Wellington Boots smiled a sneaky cat-smile. He might help, if it wasn't too much work.

"You'll trip him up if he tries to get away, won't you?" she whispered, walking over to Hank's paddock.

The white elephant winked one blue eye.

He would help Selina too.

Selina began to rake Hank's paddock. With each stroke she got closer and closer to the children's zoo. Hank followed her.

The thief turned round and saw her. Selina pretended to be raking very hard.

Out of the corner of her eye she saw him tuck another rabbit under his coat. He must have very big pockets, she thought.

Suddenly the thief moved. He was walking away from the children's zoo.

"Come on, Boots!" yelled Selina.

She ran to the thief and tried to grab him by the coat. He was too strong for her and pulled himself away. Mr Wellington Boots didn't want to be trodden on. He thought of a better idea than tripping up the thief.

Selina shouted for the keeper over by the sea-lions' lake. She shouted for the other keepers who were having their tea. But they were all a long way away. By the time they got to her the thief would have escaped with the rabbits.

But Hank the white elephant was ready for him. He coiled his long trunk round the thief's leg and pulled him over.

Then something very strange happened.

Six large dead fish fell out of the thief's pockets. They were very old fish. The smell

was horrible! The thief held his nose, and three more fish fell out of his sleeves. They were very old too. The smell was digusting!

The keeper could smell them as he ran from the sea-lions' lake.

The rest of the keepers smelled them. It spoiled their tea. They came out to find out what the stink was.

"He's stolen the chinchillas!" explained Selina.

The zoo thief couldn't believe he had his pockets full of smelly fish. He had to think fast. "I thought the fish were spare," he said. "I took them for my cat. I don't know anything about chinchillas. Look."

He pulled out several smelly fish tails from his left boot, and four fish heads from his right boot.

"Oh, Boots," said Selina. "I think we've made a mistake."

"Pooh!" said the keepers. "What a stink! Pick up those revolting things and put them in the bin," they shouted. One of the keepers picked up the brush they used for cleaning cages. "You'll have to clean up the smell," he said.

Mr Wellington Boots yawned – a wide, pink yawn.

The zoo thief thought he had got away with it. But when he picked up the penguins' fish bucket he yelled and dropped it. It was full of furry, squirmy, chinchilla rabbits.

"So you don't know anything about chinchillas, eh?" said the keepers.

The zoo thief tipped the chinchillas out of the bucket.

"Don't let them escape!" shouted Selina. "We'll never catch them if they burrow into the ground."

The zoo thief thought *he* would escape now that everyone was running about after the rabbits. But Hank put a very large foot on top of his coat to stop him from running away.

Lots of zoo visitors came to see what all the noise was about. They helped to catch the rabbits. Selina caught five chinchillas and put them back in their cages. The elephant keeper caught another seven. But it was

Hank who caught the last one. He kept his
foot on the thief's coat, so that he didn't get
away, then with his long trunk he picked up
the last chinchilla rabbit and gave it to one of
the keepers.

Another of the keepers ran to phone the police, and the thief was taken away. He still smelled of rotten fish.

"Well done, Hank," said the keepers.

Mr Wellington Boots thought he ought to have been thanked as well, but nobody listened to him.

The director of the zoo was very pleased. "I'm glad you asked us to have Hank," he said. He invited them to a special tea the next day so that he and his keepers could say thank you properly.

Dad and Mum and Peter and Mr Wellington Boots were invited too. Peter said it would be hay and raw meat, but it wasn't. Hank had extra hay, but the children had sandwiches and cake and ice-cream and all the things they liked best.

Mr Wellington Boots was given a whole pail full of fish, all to himself.

It was a funny thing, but he didn't feel very keen on fish after catching the zoo thief.

# 3. Mr Wellington Boots' Holiday

## Chapter 1

It was holiday time again and the family was trying to find Mr Wellington Boots.

Mr Wellington Boots hated being left behind. He knew he would like playing on the beach just as much as Selina. He didn't see why he should go to the cattery. Ordinary cats went to catteries, but not a magic cat like him.

So he hid behind the bushes in the garden, but Selina knew where to look for him there. When Mr Wellington Boots heard her coming he ran and hid in the shed by the rakes and hoes. Peter knew where to look for him there so he ran and hid in the cupboard under the stairs. Dad knew where to look for him there so he ran and hid in the garage, under the car. Mum knew where to look for him there so he ran into his cat basket. No one thought of looking for him there.

The family had rented a cottage, right by the sea. They collected their spades and buckets and fishing nets and packed them into the boot of the car. Mum remembered the sleeping bags. Peter remembered the cases. Dad remembered the picnic basket, at the last minute.

"But where is that cat!" shouted Dad. "How can I take him to the cattery if he isn't here?"

"Why can't he come with us?" asked Selina. "He's a very good cat."

"You can't take cats to the seaside, stupid," said Peter.

"Mr Wellington Boots is different," said Selina.

Mum and Dad agreed that he was a different cat, but that didn't help find him.

"Can he come if we do find him?" asked Selina.

"Of course not," said Dad. "I've booked him in at the cattery."

But they still couldn't find Mr Wellington Boots. Mum gave Mrs Speed a key and asked if she would feed the cat while they were away. Dad had to ring the cattery to cancel Mr Wellington Boots' holiday. Selina went to the zoo to say goodbye to Hank. She promised to bring the keepers some seaside rock.

When they were all ready to go, Mr Wellington Boots climbed out of his cat basket and into the picnic basket. Nobody

saw him. Dad put the picnic basket in the back seat of the car with Selina and Peter. It was a tight squeeze.

Not far down the road a funny noise came from the engine.

"Oh, no, not already!" said Dad. He stopped the car and raised the bonnet to have a look.

Mr Wellington Boots smiled a sneaky cat-smile in the picnic basket.

"I think I've found the trouble," said Dad. He brought out three bottles of milk from under the bonnet. "Who put them there?" he said, glaring at Peter.

"Not me," said Peter.

"Not me," said Selina.

"It must have been someone," said Dad. "We don't need that much milk."

He put the bottles in the back seat with Selina, Peter and the picnic basket. It was a very tight squeeze.

Dad drove on. A little bit further down the road another funny noise came from the engine.

"Oh, no, not again," said Dad.

He stopped the car and Mum opened the bonnet to have a look. Inside were six tins of cat food.

"Selina, you knew we couldn't bring Mr Wellington Boots," said Mum. "We can drink up the milk but nobody wants cat-food sandwiches."

"But it wasn't me," said Selina.

"Nor me," said Peter.

Mum put the tins on the back seat with Selina, Peter, the picnic basket and the three bottles of milk. It was a very, very tight squeeze.

Further on it was time to stop for their picnic.

"There, Dad!" shouted Selina. "That's a good place."

"Too late, I've gone past it now," said Dad, and drove on.

Ten minutes later Peter shouted, "There, Dad!"

"There's somebody right on my tail. I can't stop now," said Dad, and drove on.

Suddenly there was a funny noise from the engine.

Dad stopped in a hurry, and four cars hooted behind him. "I suppose we'll find the cat basket wrapped round the engine now," said Dad crossly.

Peter lifted the bonnet. "There's nothing here except the engine," he said.

Dad looked as well. Peter was right. There was only an engine.

"What a lovely place for a picnic," said Mum. It was the best of all. They had stopped by a wood, with a space to park the car and plenty of places to walk.

The children ran into the trees and found a grassy glade to have their picnic.

Dad brought out the picnic basket, and they spread out the rug on the grass.

"I'm looking forward to this," said Dad.

He opened the basket. There was no

picnic inside, only Mr Wellington Boots,
purring gently.

Dad was not pleased. "Where's my
picnic?" he asked. "How can I drive all the
way to the seaside without food? And whose
idea was this?"

"Not mine," said Peter.

"Not mine," said Selina.

But she was pleased. Mr Wellington Boots
would have to come on holiday with them

73

after all. It was too far to take him back home, and Dad had cancelled the cattery.

Mum looked in the boot. One of the sleeping bags had come unrolled.

"What a funny place to pack a picnic," said Mum. She took out the boxes of sandwiches, the apples and bananas, and several bags of prawn cocktail crisps from the unrolled sleeping bag.

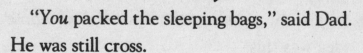

"*You* packed the sleeping bags," said Dad. He was still cross.

But Mr Wellington Boots didn't care. He ate some cat food and drank some milk. Then he went to sleep in the picnic basket.

## Chapter 2

Mum and Dad did not enjoy their holiday. It rained on the first day. It rained on the second day. The sun shone on the third day and they went down to the beach. Dad's nose got sunburnt. On the fourth day Mum's back got sunburnt. Mr Wellington Boots decided he didn't like sand. It got into his fur.

But Peter and Selina went down to the

beach every day and swam in the sea. They were enjoying their holiday.

On the last day Dad's nose had turned brown and Mum's back had stopped feeling sore. Dad woke up early and woke Mum. "It looks nice. Let's go for a trip on the ferry," he said. "We'll take the camera and a picnic."

The ferry went across the bay from the harbour to Cliff Tops.

Mum yawned and tried to go back to sleep, but Dad wanted to have a good end to this holiday.

Mum made them all eat breakfast and make sandwiches before they went out.

"Don't roll the sandwiches in a sleeping bag this time!" joked Dad.

"It wasn't me," said Mum.

"Nor me," said Selina.

"Nor me," said Peter.

"Then it must have been the cat, because

it wasn't me," laughed Dad.

"Has somebody fed him?" asked Mum.
"We'd better shut him in the cottage. We
don't want him to run away on our last day."

So they shut Mr Wellington Boots in the
cottage and went down to the harbour to
catch the ferry to Cliff Tops.

Mr Wellington Boots didn't think being shut in a holiday cottage was a good place for him to spend his holiday. He found a window open in the bathroom and jumped out. He followed the family down to the beach, making sure they didn't see him.

The harbour was full of fishing boats and seagulls.

"Look, there's a catamaran," said Peter. It was a boat with two hulls, like two canoes stuck together. "We should have brought Boots after all. It's just the boat for him."

Mr Wellington Boots sniffed at the catamaran. He thought it was a very boring boat. The fishing boats smelled much better. A seagull zoomed down like a fighting aeroplane and chased him off.

"Look – there's a cat just like Boots," said Selina.

"It can't be," said Peter. "We've shut him in the cottage."

"Anyway, Boots wouldn't let a seagull chase him away," said Selina.

They watched the ferry come in, so they didn't see Mr Wellington Boots smile his sneaky cat-smile. But they did see a whole lot of model aeroplanes suddenly fly round the fishing boat aerials, chasing the seagulls away.

"There must be a model aeroplane club here," said Dad.

"I can't see anybody working them," said Peter. He looked round, but it was time to board the ferry.

It wasn't a big ferry. There was only room for about twenty people. There was a cabin where the engine was, but the people had to sit out in the open on wooden seats. Above the engine cabin was a tall mast with a flag on top.

"No cats," said the ferry man. He could see Mr Wellington Boots waiting to get on.

"Of course not," said Dad. He thought Mr Wellington Boots was safely locked inside the holiday cottage.

The ferry man was having a bit of trouble with the model aeroplanes. They kept flying round his engine cabin so that he couldn't see to steer the boat out of the harbour.

Mr Wellington Boots jumped on to the ferry while everyone was bothered about the model aeroplanes. He hid under a seat.

"Drat these models!" shouted the ferry man. He grumbled to the boy who helped him collect the fares, "How do they expect me to do my job?"

Dad went up to the front of the boat and tried to see who was operating the models. Peter went to the back and tried to see from there.

Selina suddenly saw Mr Wellington Boots under a seat. She sat on the seat and put down a hand to tickle him under the chin.

"How did you get out, Boots?" she whispered.

Mr Wellington Boots yawned a wide, pink yawn, and the model aeroplanes flew away. The seagulls came back, but Mr Wellington Boots was under the seat and they couldn't see him.

"Funny," said Dad. "I couldn't see who was working them."

The ferry man glared at Dad as if it was all his fault. He pulled a knob in the engine and the ferry boat made a noise like a lorry. It churned up a lot of oily water, and began to move out of the harbour.

The seagulls shrieked and squawked round the boat.

"This is nice," said Mum. She put on her sunglasses.

"Wait a minute," said Dad. "We're going the wrong way."

The ferry was going out to sea, and not to Cliff Tops at all. They had caught the wrong boat. It was going to the island several miles away. It was a much longer trip and would be more expensive.

The boy who helped the ferry man came round to collect the fares. Dad felt in his pockets. He hoped he had enough money.

"Did you bring your handbag?" he asked

Mum. "Did you remember your pocket money?" he asked Peter and Selina.

None of them had.

Dad counted his money.

"Just as well I've got enough," he grumbled.

## Chapter 3

There were big waves outside the bay. Water began to splash over one side of the boat.

Some of the passengers put up umbrellas.

"I can see you've made this trip before," said Dad to them.

Selina and Peter were getting wet.

"Come over to this side," said Mum. She moved so that they could both get in. But Mr

Wellington Boots was still on the splashy side of the boat, and he just hated water!

"Let me take a photo," said Peter. He focused the camera at the waves and at the people with their umbrellas. But there was something else in the viewfinder. "It's Boots!" he cried.

"Don't be silly," said Dad. "We've locked the cat in the cottage."

"It looks just like Boots," said Mum.

"It can't be. It must be the ship's cat," said Dad. He settled down to watch the island come nearer.

Poor Mr Wellington Boots was getting wetter and wetter. He crawled out from the seat on the splashy side of the boat, but the deck was covered in sea water. The ferry man steered the boat right into an enormous wave. Water flew up over the engine cabin. The passengers with umbrellas moved them just in time to catch the water. Mr Wellington Boots didn't see the wave coming, but the wave saw him. He felt the water slop right into his face. It was like being hit with a hundred wet fish all at the same time.

The cat streaked right up to the top of the flag mast. He clung there, holding on to the flag by his claws, and yowled.

"Help!" shouted Selina. "That's my cat!"

"That's why I said No Cats," shouted the ferry man. "Bring it down before it rips my flag to shreds."

"We've got to rescue him!" cried Selina.

More waves splashed into the boat. The passengers began to panic.

"Help! There's too much water in this boat!" shouted one of the passengers. She pushed her umbrella at the waves to try and stop them coming in.

"We're sinking!" yelled another passenger. He took his swimming trunks out of his bag, ready to swim for it.

The boy who collected the money called the lifeboat over the radio. "SOS! We're drowning!"

Then Mr Wellington Boots gave an immense yowl and a huge fish like a small whale flopped into the boat. It opened its mouth and all the people shrieked. The big fish sucked in the water that was sloshing about in the boat. It sucked in one of the umbrellas too. Then Mr Wellington Boots hissed and the big fish slurped out of the boat again.

"I thought we were done for then!" said Dad.

"Save my cat!" shouted Selina. "Hang on tight, Boots!"

Peter took a photograph of Mr Wellington Boots hanging on tight, high up on the flag mast. Selina tried to climb the mast to rescue him.

"Get down!" said Dad.

"What can we do?" cried Mum.

But there was another boat, coming nearer and nearer. It was the lifeboat.

"Help!" cried Selina. "Please rescue my cat!"

"Cat?" said the lifeboatmen. "We came to rescue *you* from drowning, not a cat."

"We're okay – a big fish came and sucked all the water up," said Peter, but the lifeboatmen didn't believe him. When the ferry man told them the same story they said he must have been out in the sun too long.

"Please rescue my cat," said Selina. "He's frightened."

The smallest lifeboatman climbed up the mast to rescue Mr Wellington Boots. Boots put out all his claws to scratch him.

"Don't scratch, Boots. He's coming to help you."

Mr Wellington Boots wasn't too sure about that. But he only gave the lifeboatman a very small scratch, just to show him who was boss.

"Thank you very much!" said Selina. She cuddled a very wet Mr Wellington Boots.

"Don't mention it," said the lifeboatmen. "But don't bring cats out to sea again."

"I *said* No Cats," said the ferry man.

The lifeboatmen sailed away to rescue someone else. The children waved, and Mr Wellington Boots waved too.

## Chapter 4

At last the boat stopped at the island and all the people got off. Peter carried the camera and took pictures of the island. Selina cuddled Mr Wellington Boots.

Dad picked up the picnic basket but he tripped on the gang plank and suddenly he didn't have the picnic basket any more. He fished it out of the sea with the end of somebody's umbrella, but it was too late. The apples and bananas were all right, but the sandwiches were very soggy.

"I don't like salty wet sandwiches," said Peter.

Mr Wellington Boots decided he wouldn't help this time. He had had enough of magic for one day. He yawned, showing his pink mouth and his spiky teeth. Then he went to sleep in Selina's arms and refused to wake up.

Dad found a café. "This is becoming an expensive day," he grumbled.

They had to wait in the rain for the ferry to go back again. It was too expensive to stay in the café all the time. Selina tucked Mr Wellington Boots inside her jumper, but he got wet all the same.

And Dad had to pay for the cat to travel on the boat. Both ways.

They arrived back at the cottage. Mum

turned on the fire and Dad made some tea.

"Next time we come on holiday that animal is going to the cattery," said Dad. "I don't care how long it takes to find him."

Mr Wellington Boots didn't argue. This was the last time he would take his family on holiday!

"It will be nice to be home," said Selina.

The family agreed with her. Mum looked forward to weeding the garden. Peter and Dad looked forward to watching a football match on TV. Selina looked forward to the zoo, and going to help with Hank.

But Mr Wellington Boots didn't look forward to anything. He was warm and full of food already. He didn't mind where he was, so long as it stayed that way!

The End